ARCHBISHOP TUTU OF SOUTH AFRICA

Judith Bentley

ENSLOW PUBLISHERS, INC.

Bloy St. & Ramsey Ave. P.O. Box 38
Box 777   Aldershot
Hillside, N.J. 07205 Hants GU12 6BP
U.S.A.   U.K.

Library of Congress Cataloging-in-Publication Data

Bentley, Judith.
  Archbishop Tutu of South Africa.

  Bibliography: p.
  Includes index.
  1. Summary: Traces the life of the clergyman from his early years in Klerksdorp, South Africa, to his current crusade for peace in that strife-torn country.
  1. Tutu, Desmond. 2. Church of the Province of Southern Africa—Bishops—Biography—Juvenile literature. 3. Anglican Communion—South Africa—Bishops—Biography— Juvenile literature. 4. Race relations—Religious aspects—Christianity— Juvenile literature. 5. South Africa—Race relations— Juvenile literature. [1. Tutu, Desmond. 2. Clergy. 3. South Africa—Biography]
  I. Title
  BX5700.6.Z8T873   1988   283'.3 [B] [92]   88-410
  ISBN 0—89490—180—X

Printed in the United States of America

10 9 8 7 6 5 4 3 2

Illustration Credits

A/P Wide World Photos, pp. 45, 69, 71, 74, 76, 78, 80, 81; Courtesy of I.D.A.F., pp. 21, 24, 33, 41, 43, 53, 55, 58, 62, 65; U.N. Photo, 164 865/Milton Grant, p. 3; U.N. Photo 155597/ Marc Vanappelghem, p. 15; U.N. Photo, 151906, p. 30; U.N. Photo 134820, p. 31; U.N. Photo 151707, p. 61; WCC Photo: Peter Williams, p. 83.

ACKNOWLEDGMENTS

Communication between the United States and the Republic of South Africa is not easy. I would like to thank the following people for their help in putting this book together: Naomi Tutu and Corbin Seavers (Bishop Tutu Refugee Fund in Hartford, Conn.) Archbishop Desmond Tutu and Mrs. Leah Tutu, Rt. Rev. Trevor Huddleston, C.R., Dr. William Scott (Oberlin College), Kim Irving (UPI, South Africa), Congressman Mike Lowry, Mrs. Sylvia Morrison, Matt Esau, Thenmbi Sekgathane, Rev. Cabell Tennis (St. Mark's Cathedral, Seattle), Dr. Hulme Siwundhla (University of Washington).

To my parents

Contents

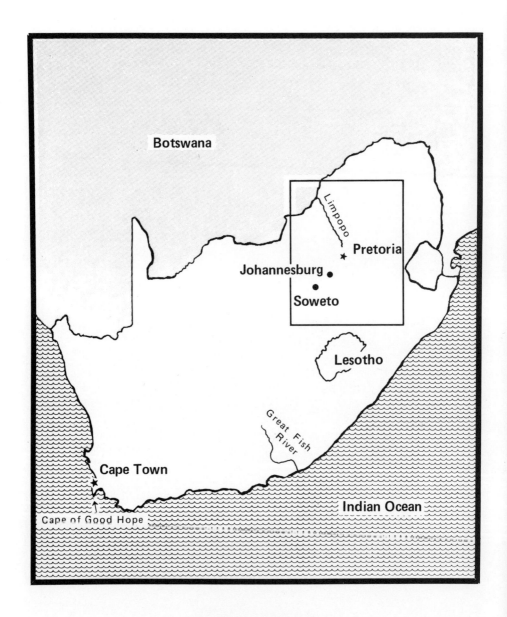

South Africa

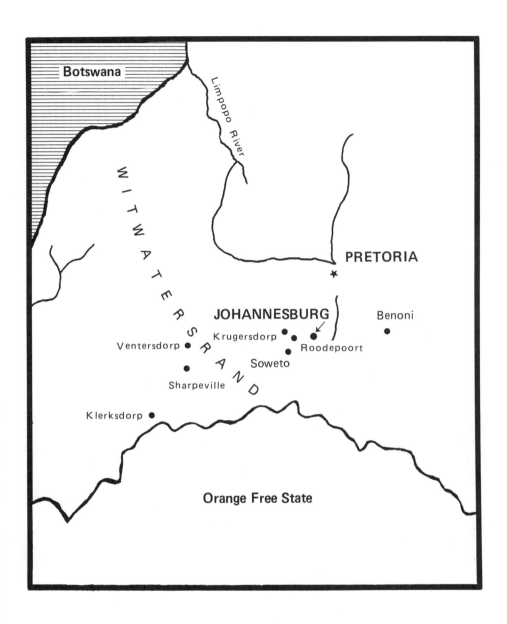

Johannesburg

1

Black Boy and White

On a ridge of mountains in South Africa known as the Witwatersrand, trucks dump pulverized ore from the gold mines onto ever-growing piles. From those dumps, fine yellow sand blows down into the nearby towns and cities, into the shops and houses, into people's eyes and into their food.

The sand blows alike on the white South Africans in the towns and on the black South Africans outside of the towns in areas called locations. The locations are rows and rows of boxlike houses with dirt in the front yard, dirt in the side yard, and dirt that turns to mud in the streets. When the wind is not blowing sand, a cloud of smoke hangs over the houses from the braziers, or stoves, used for cooking and heating.

Young Desmond Tutu left such a location one day in the 1930s to bicycle into the town of Ventersdorp to buy his father a newspaper. As his legs pedaled steadily, he encountered a group of white boys.

"Pik!" they called out to him. "Pik-swart!"

Desmond was puzzled by the taunt. He understood most of Afrikaans, the language spoken by descendants of the

Dutch in South Africa. But why would the boys be calling him a pick—a garden tool?

The tone of their voices left no doubt of their intent, however, and he beat a hasty retreat. From a safe distance, he hollered back, "You graaf!"

Graaf means "shovel" in Afrikaans; it was the only word he could think of to say "The same to you!"

Later, he realized what they had called him. *Pik* can mean garden pick, or it can mean black. *Pik-swart* means very black, as in *pitch-black*. The insult was the South African equivalent of *nigger*.

That exchange was Desmond Tutu's first experience of the hostility between blacks and whites in South Africa, a country where the descendants of Europeans are 15 percent of the population and native Africans are 73 percent of the population. (The others are Asians or Coloureds, meaning people of mixed race.) Because he had always lived in the locations, Desmond knew very few whites.

His parents knew more of the world and had already developed their ways of living with the hostility. Desmond's father, Zachariah Tutu, was a very tall, bald-headed, imposing man. He was a Xhosa (pronounced "Koe'-suh"), a member of a tribe that had warred fiercely with the white settlers less than a century before. Zachariah still had some of the Xhosa fierceness. He could be "like a Hitler in the home," Desmond's sister Sylvia remembers.

Desmond's mother, Aletta, was of the Tswana tribe, which had a more peaceful reputation. Aletta always stood up for the person who was getting the worst in an argument, even if she had to change sides in the middle. Besides her compassionate nature, she passed on to Desmond a large nose and short height. She and Zachariah were an unusual match, in stature and in temperament.

Their ancestors, in turn, had different experiences of the coming of white settlers to South Africa. Both the Xhosa and the Tswana had been migrating southward toward the tip of the African continent for centuries. About 1300 they crossed the Limpopo River (a northern boundary of modern South Africa). Two hundred years later they had reached the Great Fish River, which flows into the Indian Ocean. There the Xhosa met the Boers.

The Boers (literally, "farmers") were descendants of Dutchmen, Germans, and Huguenots who had been dropped off at the Cape of Good Hope in the 1600s. Their job was to supply meat to ships sailing to India and the Far East. At first the Europeans traded with the Africans for cattle, but soon they began raising their own cattle, bringing wives from Europe, farming, and moving along the coast, looking for more farmland and meadowland.

The Xhosa had also taken up farming and raising cattle, and eventually both Boers and Xhosa wanted the same land. They began raiding and killing each other's cattle, starting a series of wars that lasted 100 years. By 1880, the Xhosa had been defeated.

The Tswana, Aletta Tutu's tribe, did not fight with the Boers but asked the British for protection. The British had also come to the Cape in the late 1700s, to start a base for their navy. When the British arrived, the Boers undertook a Great Trek, moving farther inland in ox wagons to get away from the newcomers. A hardy, pioneer people, they felt they were in a struggle for survival with both the Africans and the British.

As they trekked, the Boers threatened the Tswana, who had never been a nation of warriors. The Tswana settled disputes through negotiation and compromise, so they asked the British trading agents and missionaries who had settled among them for protection. The British fought a successful war with the Boers between 1898 and 1901 and dominated the country politically for the next forty-seven years. They never granted political rights to the Tswana and Xhosa.

Thus Desmond's ancestors had tried both fighting and negotiating as ways of living with the Europeans. Many also converted to their religion. After the Xhosa were defeated, some of them clung to their tribal ways and became known as the "red" people because they continued to wear wool blankets dyed red with ocher (clay colored by iron oxide). Zachariah's people had become "school" Xhosa, choosing to become educated in the mission schools established by missionaries. Their decision to try to get along with the Europeans in South Africa meant that Desmond would have a Western, Christian education.

Zachariah had ambitions for himself and his children. He had sent Desmond to town for a newspaper because the locations had no shops and he wanted to be able to read about the world. An educated man who pursued college degrees throughout his life, he was headmaster of a primary school for black children. He had high hopes that education would earn his children a better way of life, too.

The Tutus' first daughter had survived, but two sons had already died in infancy when a third son was born on October 7, 1931. Zachariah chose his name carefully and hopefully: Desmond, an English name meaning "courageous."

Courage was needed, for Desmond was a sickly baby. A few months after his birth, he developed an illness that made him cry constantly for food. After a month he became so still that the doctors thought he was dead, and his father said, "I don't think there's any life in him."

When the baby miraculously recovered, his granny declared his name should be Mpilo—a word from her Sotho language meaning "life." Thus Mpilo was added to Desmond: Desmond Mpilo Tutu. Combined in the two names were the two worlds Desmond would live in: British schools and churches, African homes and traditions.

Many African families were separated when the fathers went to work in the mines or the cities, but the Tutus were able to stay together when Desmond was young. The parents and three children, including Desmond's older sister Sylvia and younger sister Gloria, lived near the mission schools where Zachariah taught. Aletta took in laundry to supplement her husband's meager salary as a teacher so the children had enough food to eat and clothes to wear.

Many black men who work on contract in the mines or cities must live in dormitories such as this. They are separated from their families for a year or more at a time.

There were times, however, when the children were left alone, with Sylvia in charge. One day when Aletta had gone out, Desmond strayed too close to the brazier, and his pajamas caught fire. He was so frightened that he ran amok, and Sylvia had to grab him. She patted the fire onto his flesh to put it out, which made the burn worse but saved his life.

Life for other children in the location was even more precarious. Desmond was a child during the Depression, a time when food and jobs were scarce for many people. Many black people had come to the cities and towns looking for work, especially in the gold mining towns along the Witwatersrand, or Rand, as it was called for short. From fields around towns like Klerksdorp (where Desmond was born) and Ventersdorp (where he lived from ages seven to twelve), South Africa mines more gold than any other country in the world.

But unlike the sand from the dumps, little of the gold filters down to black South Africans. Many of the children in the locations were hungry. Desmond had seen them scavenging for food white children had thrown into the rubbish bins behind their school. White children received free sandwiches and fruit at school, but they often preferred what their mothers had sent in their lunch boxes. Only a third of the black children even went to school, and they received no free lunch. Desmond thought it unfair that children who were already well off were fed, while children who needed food most were not.

But in most things, Desmond did not find the separation of the races particularly odd. As a child who went to church every Sunday, he thought, "Well, this is how God has ordered the world. Your place in the world is this part and you will take it."

Besides miners, factory workers, and domestic workers, preachers and teachers were the most common models Desmond saw of black people who had taken their place in the world. One of the most respected men in each community was the umfundisi, or preacher.

Such a person was Zachariah Sekgaphane, a gentle and caring umfundisi who served Desmond's parish. When Father Sekgaphane visited the farm outstations in the parish, he would take several young boys along to serve as altar boys, including Desmond.

The visit of the umfundisi was an important occasion, and the people on the farms would prepare their best food—perhaps a chicken—and dance attendance on him. Before Father Sekgaphane ever sat down for a meal, however, he would come out "and see that we lesser mortals had been catered to," Desmond remembers. Someday, he thought, he would like to be like this man.

2

Madibane High

When Desmond started school at age seven, his parents expected him to excel. For white children, free schooling was provided by the government. But the only schools for black children were mission schools started by the churches, and they had to charge fees. Desmond's parents worked hard to pay the school fees for their three children.

In 1938 Desmond enrolled at St. Ansgar's, a Swedish mission boarding school in another town along the Rand. African children had traditionally learned from their parents how to herd cattle, plant corn, cook, and do other chores. But the education Desmond received was a British, Christian education. He was taught in English, rather than the Sotho language spoken at home. He studied European history and read English poetry.

Right away his classmates could tell that Desmond was smart—smart enough not to believe everything he heard and read. When his teacher said that Victoria Falls, the most magnificent waterfall in Africa, was "discovered" by a white man named David Livingston, Desmond wondered if the native people living around the waterfall hadn't noticed it, too!

Likewise, he found a strange choice of words when the history book described conflicts between the Xhosa and the white colonists in South Africa. The book always said, "The Xhosa *stole* the colonists' cattle," but "the colonists *captured* [or *recaptured*] the Xhosa's cattle."

In church, too, Desmond heard a European viewpoint. The Afrikaners, descendants of the Dutch who had come to South Africa in the 1600s, believed that they had found a promised land and that the native Africans should work for them. The British missionaries, in contrast, preached equality: "All are one in Christ." From what he heard in British churches, Desmond began to doubt that God had, in fact, ordered the separation of the races and a superior place for whites.

One priest in particular, a white man who made such an impression on Desmond that he later named his first son after him, encouraged those doubts. Desmond met Father Trevor Huddleston in a neighborhood in Johannesburg called Sophiatown.

All along the Rand in the early 1940s, black people were moving to Johannesburg, the city of gold. White men were fighting in South Africa's army in World War II, and black workers were needed in the mines and factories and in jobs like digging tunnels and roads.

Johannesburg was not a very lovely place. It was a brash, prosperous city which had grown rapidly when gold was discovered on the Rand in 1886. It was also a city of contrasts: gleaming white houses with swimming pools for the whites in the city and suburbs; government-built concrete boxes or ramshackle huts for the newly arrived black workers in the "temporary" locations or townships.

There was one "black spot" in the city, however, where blacks could own their own houses and land. An entrepreneur

Desmond grew up on locations such as this outside of the prosperous towns and cities along the Rand.

had bought the land for a white suburb, but the city council decided to build sewage disposal plants and the first black township nearby. When the plots wouldn't sell to whites, they were sold to blacks, Coloureds, and Asians instead. There, within bicycling distance of downtown, was the multiracial neighborhood known as Sophiatown.

As Desmond turned twelve, in 1943, his family was drawn to Johannesburg, too. Zachariah had a new teaching job just outside the city. After five years at St. Ansgar's, Desmond would go to school in Johannesburg and spend some of his teenage years in Sophiatown.

That same year the young priest Trevor Huddleston sailed from Liverpool, England, for his new assignment in Sophiatown. Twenty-nine years old, Father Huddleston was from a wealthy and well-known family in England. He had taken a vow of poverty and chastity to join the Community of the Resurrection, a religious community of monks. Very tall, with dark, short-cropped hair and black, vibrant eyes, he was eager to serve the parish of Christ the King.

Christ the King was a new cathedral which had been built high on a ridge overlooking Sophiatown. With its red brick walls and a red tin roof, Huddleston thought it looked like a "huge and holy garage." Inside was a statue of the young Christ as a black boy.

On Sundays, a thousand people would come to the eleven o'clock mass at Christ the King. Every other day of the week they came, too, with their requests to Father Huddleston: to come baptize a sick baby, to help free someone from prison, or to ask a landlord to turn the water back on. Health, food, housing, work, and trouble with the police were constant problems in Sophiatown.

From long days of trying to ease their problems, Father Huddleston became an outspoken defender of Sophiatown's residents. He raised money to feed black children; he built the only Olympic-sized swimming pool for Africans; and he started the Huddleston Jazz Band with saxophones and cornets begged from church patrons.

Desmond first saw the new priest one day when he was standing on the street with his mother. Aletta Tutu had found work as a cook at a mission school for blind children and Huddleston was acquainted with her. "I was standing with my mother one day," Desmond remembers, "when this white man in a cassock walked past and doffed his big black hat to her. I couldn't believe it—a white man raising his hat to a simple black labouring woman."

The nodding acquaintance advanced to a friendship when Desmond's sister Sylvia enrolled at St. Peter's, an integrated school run by Huddleston and the Community of the Resurrection. St. Peter's was one of the best schools in South Africa and one of the few open to blacks. Zachariah Tutu paid one pound a month out of his meager nine-pound salary so that Sylvia could go there.

As was customary, the family also switched churches when their children switched mission schools. Instead of Methodists, they became Anglicans, or members of the Church of the Province of South Africa. Father Huddleston became their parish priest.

Desmond enrolled at the only African high school for miles around, in the township the city council had built next to Sophiatown. It was named Western Native Township High School, but students thought the word *native* was racist, so they called it Madibane after its principal, Harry Madibane.

Madibane High School had one sturdy, red brick building built by the Anglicans. Students came from as far as thirty miles away, and soon it was overcrowded. Extensions were added, and classes were conducted in one big room at the

African children often walk long distances from their townships to school.

community hall. So students had to listen carefully to hear above the din.

The school had other shortcomings. There were no metric measuring devices and no science equipment. Students studied drawings in books instead of doing the experiments. But it was still a rigorous academic education in subjects like Latin, English, chemistry, physics, and mathematics.

At Madibane, Desmond continued to advance through all the standards, or steps, of the school system. Because he was very smart, he had already skipped one year. At the end of high school, he hoped to score high enough on national exams to gain admission to medical school.

Madibane was a long train ride from where his family was living, so Desmond moved in with his aunt and uncle in a closer township. Like other teenage boys, he earned money by selling peanuts at the railroad station and caddying for whites at the Killarney golf course in Johannesburg. But he still didn't have enough food or warm clothing. There was a time in the winter months when he didn't even have shoes to wear.

In the smoky, overcrowded conditions of the townships, tuberculosis was common among children. Desmond had always been frail and slim and unable to put on weight. His classmates never expected him to get anywhere in the world because he was so sickly. At the age of fourteen, he came down with tuberculosis, too.

For twenty weary months, Desmond lay in a bed in the public TB hospital for Africans. With important school exams coming up, he was frustrated at his illness and a little lonely. But Father Huddleston came to visit every week, always bringing an armload of books for the bookworm.

Huddleston saw something in Desmond. "This little boy very well could have died, but he didn't give up and he never lost his glorious sense of humor," he recalled later. The priest always left his bedside refreshed and cheered.

With the weekly visits to encourage him and his own pluck and•patience, Desmond overcame the tuberculosis. He returned to school but moved into a house next door to the priory in Sophiatown, where Father Huddleston lived. Huddleston had built the house for boys who had to travel long distances to Madibane. In the evenings, Harry Madibane would often stop by the priory to talk with Father Huddleston about his students and their prospects on the national exams.

Once back in the classroom, Desmond resolved to work even harder to go on to college. But he also kept his sense of humor; he was gaining a reputation as a very funny guy.

Mr. Madibane was very sticky with his students about two things: "keeping time" (being punctual) and having a neat appearance. Both demands were bound to give the students trouble.

When Desmond and a friend, Motlalepula Chabaku, came in late one morning, the principal asked Desmond for an explanation.

"The train left me," Desmond replied, as giggles broke out behind him in the classroom.

"The train did not leave you," the principal replied sternly. "You were late."

Mondays and Fridays were dress-up days. The girls were supposed to wear hose with seams going up the back of their legs. The boys had to wear white shirts, gray pants, ties, and socks with their shoes. Few of the students could afford such niceties, especially the hose, which got runs all the time. So the girls put Vaseline on their legs to make them look shiny and drew a line in ink down the back.

When it rained one day and all the ink ran, the girls were found out. Mr. Madibane decided to scrutinize all the students. On close inspection, Desmond was found to be wearing only one sock—on the foot he put forward—and a shirt with no back.

Desmond's sense of humor would be a blessing as he encountered more obstacles than tuberculosis. As he finished high school in 1950, he took national exams in competition with all the students in South Africa. Just as he had hoped, he scored high enough to earn admission to medical school. Medical school is expensive, however; when the time came to enroll, Desmond's family could not afford the fees.

3

Defiance Against Apartheid

Desmond was walking with his father one day on the way from the Braamfontein station in Johannesburg when they were stopped by a policeman who demanded a pass. The headmaster, a respected man in his community, had to reach into his pocket and produce his pass. The pass had Zachariah Tutu's picture and said that he had, among other things, the right to be passing through the white area of Braamfontein.

Zachariah didn't indicate to his son that he resented being stopped. He was a very strict person, and he took laws very seriously, even the pass laws. Being asked for a pass was just something that happened to you in Africa because you were black.

Desmond, however, sensed humiliation. "What that does to you and your feeling as a human being is horrible. . . . I knew there wasn't a great deal I could do, but it just left me churned . . . poor man, what he must have been going through, being humiliated in the presence of his son."

Carrying a pass was just one of the restrictions placed on blacks through a series of laws establishing and maintaining a system called apartheid. Apartheid, meaning "apart-ness," was designed to keep the races separate and the whites in a superior position. Many of the laws had been passed in 1948, just before Desmond finished high school.

That year a political party dominated by the Afrikaners had won a majority of seats in the country's Parliament. The Nationalists, as the party was called, added many new restrictions to those that already existed for blacks. In addition to being forbidden to vote, to live in white areas, to strike, to buy land or houses outside tribal reserves, they were also forbidden to move around freely, to marry whites, or to protest in a radical fashion. The laws established segregated buses, libraries, restaurants, theaters, drinking fountains, and public bathrooms. When the Nationalists were finished, the volume of sixty-four basic apartheid laws weighed five pounds in English and another five pounds in Afrikaans. They said in many

Under the apartheid system put into law in 1948, whites, blacks, Coloureds, and Asians were separated socially, economically, and geographically.

30

different ways that black people were allowed in the cities only to work for whites.

When he turned eighteen, Desmond, too, had to apply for a pass, an experience one African writer said "cut through me like a knife." The pass classified Desmond as "native, tribal origin Xhosa." As long as he was going to school or working in Johannesburg, he could stay. But if he was ever out of work or in trouble with the law, the tribal classification would be used to "return" him to a Xhosa homeland—the Transkei—where he had never lived. The homelands are areas set aside for the "separate development" of blacks.

The lengths to which apartheid was carried were almost funny. Disappointed that he could not go to medical school, Desmond decided to become a teacher instead. He enrolled at Pretoria Bantu Normal College, a segregated teachers college for Bantus, or black Africans. At Pretoria Normal, Des-

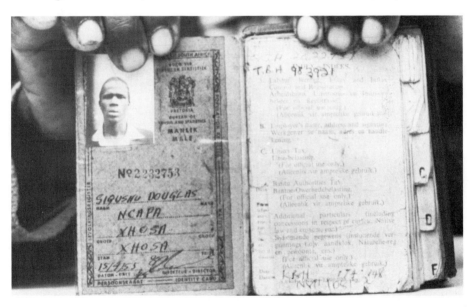

All Black Africans aged 18 and over must carry a pass book with their picture and tribal identification (which is Xhosa in this example).

mond was assigned to live in a round hut, which was supposed to make him feel at home. "They said we ought to develop along our own lines," he recalls with an unbelieving snort. "Living in rectangular buildings was Western and, I suppose, not good for our black psyches."

Desmond left Sophiatown for the round huts in Pretoria in 1950, just as protest against the new apartheid laws began. The Anglican church, especially, was speaking out against apartheid. On Sunday mornings at Christ the King, Father Huddleston preached in his sermons that all men are made in "the image and likeness of God" and that white supremacy is un-Christian.

Sitting in the congregation were young black men who would spend their lives opposing apartheid. One was Oliver Tambo, who had been a brilliant student at St. Peter's and then come back to teach math and science. Tambo and a student he had met in college, Nelson Mandela, led the African National Congress (ANC), the main protest organization, for the next thirty-five years.

Tambo and Mandela's first major action with the ANC was to organize a Defiance Campaign against the new laws. For a few months in 1952, thousands of blacks defied some of the new laws, moving around without their passes, staying out past curfew and using the "Europeans Only" drinking fountains. Eight thousand people were arrested, but the campaign ended in riots, without any change in the law.

Desmond was not a political activist at the time of the defiance campaign. At school in Pretoria, the seat of the white government, he was a student teacher. But he came down to Johannesburg one day with a team to debate the Jan Hofmeyr School of Social Work. Nelson Mandela was the judge of the debate.

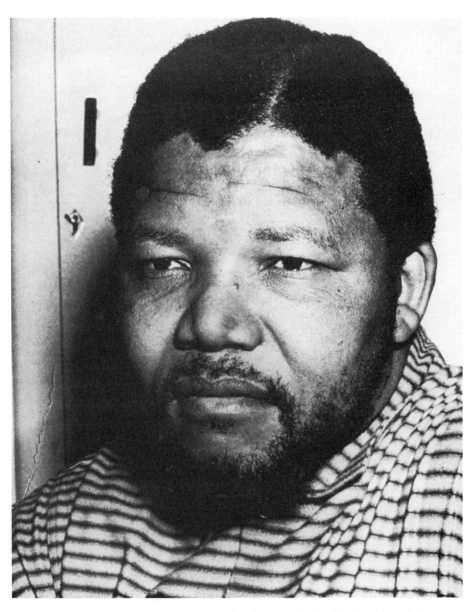

Nelson Mandela protested apartheid through his leadership of the African National Congress. He was sentenced to life imprisonment in 1964 for his actions.

Desmond immediately noticed an unusual quality in Mandela. "He had what we call in our language 'shadow'—substance, presence. He was regal." Mandela was, in fact, the son and heir of a Tembu chief. He had run away from an arranged marriage and decided he would never be the chief of a tribe that was not free. Years later, when Mandela was in prison and Tambo in exile, Tutu would take up their cause.

Apartheid was already beginning to eat away at Desmond, as the pass incident with his father revealed. He finished his teacher's training and a correspondence degree from the University of Johannesburg in 1954. Then he returned to Madibane High School in the fall to teach. There he soon found his own reason for defiance.

As a teacher, Mr. Tutu wore two socks and a whole white shirt, for he was in a privileged position. For one thing, he carried an "exemption pass," which showed that he was exempt from carrying a regular pass. The pay was low, however; since teaching was one of the few professions open to educated Africans, schools could always find qualified applicants willing to work for low salaries.

Tutu had much he wanted to share with the students at Madibane from his own reading and education, but his task became harder each year he taught. The books provided by the government gave only the European side of African history. Grammar books contained sentences like "The Kaffir [a derogatory word for a black African] has stolen a knife" and "That is a lazy Kaffir." The African characters in literature were often savages or blundering idiots.

Since the defiance campaign had failed and apartheid was firmly in place, the Nationalists were determined to change African education, too. They especially wanted to reduce the influence of British schools like St. Peter's and Madibane. Dr. H. F. Verwoerd, the minister of native affairs, said the kind of education Tutu and Tambo had received was unsuitable. Blacks should have an education in "traditional Bantu culture" instead.

On the surface, Verwoerd's idea sounded reasonable. Why should African children learn about the kings of England and Canada's wheat exports? Why not be taught in their own language and learn pride in black history? But Verwoerd did not have a proud heritage in mind. Blacks would be divided up in schools according to their tribal language, so they could not unite as Africans. Subjects like math would be neglected, and most of the teaching and books would be in Afrikaans, not English.

Desmond's friend from high school, Motlalepula, had also become a teacher. She could tell what Verwoerd had in mind: "Afrikaners just wanted to train us to be raw labor, to be able to understand commands."

Teachers and students were particularly angered at the switch in languages. English is spoken by many people in the world, and they would be isolated if they learned only Afrikaans and a tribal language. Teachers began to object to what the government said they must teach. The Anglican church decided to close Madibane rather than submit to Bantu education.

Before it closed, Desmond left Madibane to teach at a high school in Munsieville, a black township outside of Krugersdorp where his parents lived. As he continued teaching, he also found a wife. Nomalizo Leah Shenxane was a friend of his sister Gloria's and a prize student of his father's. But she was "on the quiet side" and still in primary school when Desmond went to high school, so he never paid much attention to her. For her part, she thought of him as "a stuck-up headmaster's son."

His family was sitting around talking one day about whom

Desmond should marry. They pounced on Leah's name. She had become a teacher, too, and Desmond began to take notice. Gradually both changed their initial perceptions, and they were married on July 2, 1955.

Even as Desmond and Leah formed an alliance, the ANC called a congress of black, Indian, and Coloured South Africans to write a charter for a new South Africa. The weekend before Desmond and Leah were married, thousands of people milled about in Kliptown, a village southwest of Johannesburg. Father Huddleston, who was honored at the gathering, said people were "laughing, joking, giving salutes, buying tea and scones and cold drinks and pies, listening to brave speeches, and applauding the resounding clauses of the Freedom Charter." The ideas they put in the charter—such as one man, one vote; equality before the law; and equal human rights—made the charter sound like a Declaration of Independence for South Africans under apartheid.

For Desmond and Leah, the time came for more than brave words. Two years later, over the protests of Africans and Anglicans, the Bantu Education Act was going into effect in the high schools. Desmond felt he could not stomach what he would be forced to teach.

Zachariah Tutu tried to dissuade his son, suggesting that if he stayed in teaching, he would soon be head of the school. Moreover, Leah and Desmond had a one-year-old son, Trevor, and they felt the responsibilities of parenthood. His feeling that he could have "no truck with" Bantu education was stronger, however. Along with many other teachers, he and Leah resigned in protest.

With medicine and teaching both closed to him as careers, Desmond had few options left. From Father Huddleston came one more choice. His constant speaking up for the oppressed showed Desmond what a man of the church could do.

Tutu has said he had no "highfalutin reasons" for wanting to become an Anglican priest. He had not been particularly religious as a child. There were religious and compassionate models in his family and community, however—his grandfather (who had been minister of an African Ethiopian church), his mother, Father Sekgaphane, and then Father Huddleston. The granny who named him Mpilo had even dreamed he would become a priest.

Religion offered an oasis, too, in a concrete city like Johannesburg. As a youth, Desmond liked spending quiet moments in the darkened chapel at St. Mary's Cathedral. He especially enjoyed listening to the boy choristers rehearse. Even though they looked cherubic, he knew they were up to all kinds of mischief.

So at age twenty-five, Desmond saw the church as "a likely means of service." The Anglican church wanted him, too. Although most of the priests and bishops in the late 1950s were white, most of the church members were black, so the church wanted to train more African ministers. His switch to the ministry, Tutu said later, was like being "grabbed by God by the scruff of the neck in order to spread His word, whether it is convenient or not."

4

A Simple Pastor

The night before Desmond Tutu's ordination as a priest, the bishop of Johannesburg took some of the men to a confirmation service in Christ the King, the "huge and holy garage" that had overlooked Sophiatown. By December 1961, the time of Tutu's ordination, Sophiatown no longer existed. The city government had decided to remove the "black spot" so that a white suburb could be built there. Sixty thousand people had been forced from their homes at dawn and scattered to distant townships.

Father Huddleston led a resistance campaign to save Sophiatown, but it failed. Fearing Huddleston might be arrested, the Community of the Resurrection recalled him to England, and the South African government never allowed him to return.

As Desmond looked down on what had once been Sophiatown, he reacted with anger: "This was now a devastated area, with many houses razed to the ground and weeds growing rampant all over. It was so like a bombed-out area. That had been done to maintain white supremacy."

Such moments of anger strengthened Tutu's conviction that as a priest he must oppose racism and try to bring blacks and whites together. Before he could do that, however, he needed more confidence. Standing only five feet three inches tall as an adult, he had to develop a strong voice.

Two years of theological training had developed his spiritual nature. At St. Peter's Theological College, which was also a Community of the Resurrection school, the atmosphere was one of solitude and majesty and stability. Every day Tutu took communion and had frequent prayer and meditation. Some days were quiet days, when he hardly spoke at all. He began to feel fulfilled, and the rituals became part of his daily life.

His first church was St. Alban's in Daveyton, a township outside of Benoni. He served there as a licentiate and then as a deacon, the first two levels of Anglican ministry. He assumed the normal work of a parish—baptisms, marriages, funerals, Sunday school, and sermons. Those he preached in a variety of languages—Xhosa, English, Sotho, or Zulu, depending on the congregation.

A large sign near the entrance to Daveyton promised its residents a "pot of gold at the end of the rainbow." But the sign was wrong. When Sylvia visited her brother's family, she found five of them living in a damp, dirty, dark garage, which they had partitioned into two rooms with a curtain. Trevor was four years old; their first daughter, Thandeka, was three; and a baby, Naomi, had just been born.

St. Alban's members weren't any better off. Daveyton had treeless streets and dry, parched dirt "gardens" between the concrete houses. The residents worked in the factories of Benoni, an industrial area east of Johannesburg. Worse than the living and working conditions, however, were the continuing indignities of the pass laws. Every day, in townships and towns like Daveyton and Benoni, thousands of Africans were stopped, and many were arrested because they were not carrying their passes or their passes were not "in order."

Most of the leaders of the African National Congress, including Nelson Mandela, had been on trial for treason for the past four years. Another leader, Robert Sobukwe, decided to break off from the ANC to form the Pan-Africanist Congress. Sobukwe called for a nationwide protest against the pass laws, a day when all Africans would stay home from work and hand in their passes at the police stations.

Robert Sobukwe called for a day of protest against the pass laws on March 21, 1960. He was the first person to turn in his pass at the police station. He was arrested, imprisoned for nine years, and then banned from speaking in public for the rest of his life.

In a black location known as Sharpeville, south of Johannesburg, a crowd began gathering at the police station early on the morning of March 21, 1960. Workers had been told not to go to work, that something would happen at the police station. As the curious crowd of men, women, and children milled around during the morning, the police became increasingly nervous. Somehow, without ever warning the people to leave, the police opened fire. Sixty-seven people were killed and 186 were wounded. Seventy percent of them were shot from the back as they tried to run away.

The world was shocked. Black workers staged a three-week strike in protest. Tutu's superior in the church, Bishop Ambrose Reeves, visited the injured in the hospital and took statements from the victims. Reeves warned that unless the South African government's apartheid policy was abandoned, "the coming years will bring increasing strife and sorrow."

Instead of abandoning apartheid, however, the government proclaimed a state of emergency. The police were given the power to arrest and detain anyone, even without a warrant, in the interest of keeping order. The African National Congress and the Pan-Africanist Congress were banned— made illegal.

By the time Desmond was ordained a priest, many of his friends and peers had fled the country or gone underground to evade arrest. Oliver Tambo had left the country to set up the ANC in exile. Nelson Mandela, who had been acquitted of treason, went underground to continue the ANC's work within the country when it was banned. After his criticism of the Sharpeville shooting, Bishop Reeves took "voluntary exile" from the country and was deported when he tried to return.

As an atmosphere of repression surrounded him, Tutu had the opportunity to leave the country legally. He had

Bodies lay on the ground after the Sharpeville shooting in 1960. Sixty-seven people were killed by the South African police; 70% were shot from the back as they tried to run away.

taken an exam and scored higher than all other priests in South Africa, earning himself a scholarship to King's College in England. But the government was not eager to let him go. They thought traveling abroad "spoiled" Africans. Once he finally obtained a passport, Tutu discovered they were right.

Living in England for the next four years, from 1962 to 1966, was liberating. "It was marvelous," he recounts. "We didn't have to carry our passes anymore and we did not have to look around to see if we could use that bath or that exit."

Desmond began taking long walks with Leah at night just to experience the exhilaration of the free air. They would walk to Trafalgar Square and go out of their way to encounter a policeman, just to hear him say "sir."

Another favorite spot was the speaker's corner at Hyde Park. "You would stand there and hear a person saying some of the most outlandish things, and you would see a policeman next to him, not there to arrest him for what appeared to be such subversive statements but actually to protect him from people who could get incensed. How incredible!"

In England Tutu renewed his friendship with Father Huddleston and introduced his namesake, Trevor. At King's College and in the churches he served, he met other white people as individuals, not as members of a hated group. Suddenly placed in a free atmosphere, he discovered to his dismay that his own behavior was conditioned by apartheid. In dealing with whites, he tended to defer to them.

Apartheid "can cause a child of God to doubt that he or she is a child of God . . .," Tutu realized. "You come to believe what others have determined about you, filling you with self-disgust, self-contempt and self-hatred, accepting a negative self-image."

The one positive image he could remember was the day he picked up his first tattered copy of *Ebony*. The magazine described the exploits of one Jackie Robinson, who had broken into major league baseball. Tutu didn't know baseball from ping-pong, but he did know that "Robinson had made it . . . and he was black."

At King's College, Tutu was encouraged to think for himself. Now in his early thirties, he developed more confidence in his opinions. While studying for a bachelor's degree in divinity and a master's degree in theology, he began to disagree openly and vigorously with whites.

His new self-confidence was challenged when the family returned to South Africa after four years in England. Even

Tutu was educated in British mission schools in South Africa and then received advanced degrees at King's College in England in the mid-60s. Twenty years later, as Archbishop of Cape Town, he shook hands with Queen Elizabeth II at a Commonwealth Day reception.

simple tasks could lead to humiliation. When they drove Thandeka and Naomi to school in Swaziland, the Tutus had to plan bathroom stops carefully if they didn't want to use the field. After a few times when they were forced to go to the back door of restaurants, they began carrying their own food.

The Tutus' youngest daughter, Mpho, who was born in England, had a very pronounced English accent, which was embarrassing to Leah because black pride was growing in South Africa. When Mpho piped up on the train in the only language she knew, Leah explained to the other riders, "This one was born in the kitchen," implying that Leah was a maid and Mpho was born in the servants' quarters of an English-speaking home.

With his degrees in divinity and theology, Tutu became a lecturer at the Federal Theological Seminary (FEDSEM), a new seminary formed by several denominations to train African ministers. Brought together at FEDSEM, the ministers in training began asking some difficult questions. What did Christianity have to do with Africans? Is it possible to be black and Christian at the same time? Some said the white man's god had been used to tame the black people.

One of Professor Tutu's responses to their questions was humorous agreement. He liked to tell a parable of the coming of Christianity to South Africa. "When the Europeans came to South Africa they had the Bible and we had the land. Then they said, 'Let us pray.' We closed our eyes. When we opened them, we had the Bible and they had the land."

His serious answer to their questions was that the Christian gospel could inspire blacks to break out of bondage to reclaim the land, a view called black theology. Martin Luther King, Jr., was preaching the same message in the United States: Christianity sets people free, just as the Jews were freed from Egypt in the Exodus story. The Bible speaks to the poor. The God of the Bible is a god of justice, freedom, and humanity.

Near FEDSEM, at all-black Fort Hare University, students were starting a black consciousness movement that paralleled black theology. With most of the older leaders in prison or in exile, new leaders such as journalist Steve Biko were making blacks aware of their own heritage and power.

Naturally such talk began to worry the South African government. The Nationalists threatened to expropriate or take away the seminary's land. In 1974 FEDSEM was closed for a few years when the government did take the land for use by the university.

With his uncanny timing, Tutu had moved on before the seminary closed to become a lecturer at the National University of Lesotho, a small independent country completely surrounded by South Africa. Then in 1972, he was recruited for a job in England with the World Council of Churches.

Once again, the South African government didn't want to let him go. When they refused to issue a passport, a representative had to come from England to interview him and offer him the job. Finally, Tutu wrote Prime Minister John Vorster that if he didn't get a passport, Vorster would have a very bitter black on his hands. The passport was issued. Tutu had found his voice.

5

Taking Over the Controls

Tutu's new employer was the World Council of Churches (WCC), an organization representing most of the Protestant churches in the world. The WCC was very unpopular with the South African government. As part of its worldwide mission, the council was giving money to the outlawed African National Congress and Pan-Africanist Congress for medical supplies and for the families of imprisoned black leaders.

Tutu's job was associate director of the Theological Education Fund, providing money to train ministers, particularly African ministers. The family lived in London, but Tutu was in charge of the fund's work in Africa south of the Sahara—an area about twice the size of the United States. He spent much of his time traveling in Asia and Africa visiting seminaries.

Through those travels, his eyes were opened. He saw people of color taking over the leadership of churches. He saw churches responding to social problems in other countries. His confidence in himself and his pride in other Africans increased. But there was still a little worm of doubt.

Boarding a flight in Nigeria, Tutu discovered that the pilot and copilot were both black. Thrilled at first, he began shifting uneasily in his seat once the plane was airborne. "I had a nagging worry about whether we were going to make it," and he finally realized why. "Could these blacks fly this plane . . .," he wondered, "without a white person at the controls? Whether you are aware of it or not," he reflected, "somewhere inside of you, you had always been aware of white people at the controls."

As he moved in both worlds, African and European, Tutu was preparing to take charge. He was developing an ability to talk to both blacks and whites. To whites he said that a belief in racial superiority was un-Christian: "You brought us the Bible and we are taking it seriously." To Afrikaner university students who had never known many black people, he explained why blacks are angry.

To blacks he said that Christianity promised freedom and that God was on the side of the oppressed. The enemy was white supremacy, not white people. From his own experience he knew blacks must first believe in their own worth, and he made sure that message came through.

"You would come home particularly mad about something that had happened," Naomi recalls. "He'd try to calm you down. . . . Say a white person in South Africa pushes you. . . . He taught us not to answer them by pushing back. You do not lower yourself to that level . . . basically . . . there is no such thing as inherently inferior."

He also used humor to deflect racism. Whites who fear integration with blacks in South Africa ask each other what for them is the basic question: "Would you want your daughter to marry a Kaffir?" If anyone asked blacks' opinion, Tutu said, the proper retort would be, "Show us your daughter first."

Ideally he wanted blacks and whites in South Africa to

talk to each other. On his travels, he had seen the tension and violence in Jerusalem before the 1967 Six-Day War with Egypt and the rioting in the streets of Addis Ababa in 1974 before Ethiopian Emperor Haile Selassie was overthrown. What he had seen in Uganda, the Sudan, Nigeria, Biafra, Belfast, and Vietnam convinced him violence is no solution to human problems.

South Africa seemed on a collision course, however, between urban blacks and the white government. In 1975 the Anglican church was right in the middle of the conflict. The dean of Johannesburg, Gonville ffrench-Beytagh, was expelled from the country for "subversive activities." He had been convicted of encouraging antiapartheid sentiment and giving money to the families of political prisoners. His conviction seemed like a warning to other church leaders.

The diocese needed a new dean who could talk to both blacks and whites but who would also speak out against apartheid. It also needed a dean who was a South African rather than a British citizen so he couldn't be expelled. Such a person was Desmond Tutu.

Tutu was named the first black dean of Johannesburg and of St. Mary's Cathedral, the cathedral he had loved as a youth. One of his first hopes was that St. Mary's would be prayed in by all kinds of people. In a race-mad society, he thought, there was nothing more impressive than "when St. Mary's was full to overflowing with all God's children of all races."

Such mingling was rare in South Africa, however, particularly when it came to education. Tutu was not willing to impose "Bantu education" on his children, so Thandeka and Trevor would stay in England to finish school. Naomi and Mpho would go to school in Swaziland, a small, independent country surrounded by South Africa.

Housing was another matter. The dean of Johannesburg

usually lived in the "deanery," a house in a whites-only area. To live there might require permission from the government for status as an "honorary white."

Tutu had no wish to become an "honorary white." He said, "I want to live among my people and to identify with them." So the family moved to a three-bedroom cement house in Soweto.

Soweto (from *South West To*wnship) is one huge township southwest of Johannesburg, created from twenty-six smaller townships like Western, where Madibane had been. One and a half million people live there, crowded into 100,000 houses built by the government and into uncounted shanties. The area of Soweto where the Tutus lived was jokingly known as "Beverly Hills" because the houses were larger.

The standard house in the township is made out of brick or concrete blocks. It is a tiny box with two to four rooms, depending on when it was built. An average of eight to ten people live in each house. Roofs are of corrugated iron and come in three colors: yellow, green, and red. Many have no electricity or running water.

Soweto has row upon row of such houses, with very few stores or street lights and no street signs. It is said you can get lost more easily in Soweto than anywhere else in the world. A cloud of grayish brown smoke, from wood, coal, or kerosene stoves, constantly hangs over the township. The streets are unpaved, rutted, and dusty in winter and become streams during the summer rains. Children out of school play in junk heaps or on the dusty streets. Youths without jobs tinker with burned-out cars or play dice and cards.

Tutu appealed to Christians to do something about the laws that had created Soweto. As dean, he wanted to work for reconciliation between the races, but there could be no

Beside houses built by the government, Soweto is crowded with shacks built with whatever materials its residents can find.

reconciliation without justice, he said over and over again. Religion could not be separate from politics. In the Old Testament, after all, God ordered Moses to lead the Hebrews out of bondage in Egypt. "Now if God wasn't committing a political act, what else do you call helping slaves to run away?"

In the spring of 1976, trouble was brewing among angry youths in the townships. Once again, the education of black children was the issue. The government had ruled that half of all subjects in high school were to be taught in Afrikaans, instead of in English. The black consciousness movement had given students new pride in their heritage, and they did not want to learn in the language of the "baas" (boss).

Tutu and Dr. Nthato Motlana, a physician and anti-apartheid leader, walked the streets and started talking to the youths, encouraging them to avoid violence and plan only peaceful protests. But Dean Tutu also saw the reasons for their anger and believed they were just. He was very worried about what might happen.

During a three-day religious retreat that May he wrote a long letter to Prime Minister Vorster. He appealed to Vorster as a loving and caring father and husband, as a doting grandfather, as a fellow human, a Christian, and a member of a race (Afrikaner) that had once been oppressed by another (the British). He said he feared violence and bloodshed were inevitable unless something was done very soon. Tutu made three suggestions: allow blacks to become permanent residents of the cities and buy property; repeal the pass laws; and call a national convention of leaders of all races to plan an open and just society.

Vorster paid no attention to the letter.

A few weeks later, students in Soweto decided to take action by refusing to write their social studies papers in Afrikaans. The next day they boycotted classes at the Morris Isaacson School, a junior high school.

Other students joined them in the protest. On June 16, 1976, fifteen thousand schoolchildren from all over Soweto marched through the streets, waving placards made from cardboard boxes: "Down with Afrikaans" and "Afrikaans is a tribal language." As they paraded through the streets, they met a small unit of policemen. The police opened fire, shooting a thirteen-year-old boy in the back. The students rioted in response, and hundreds were killed in Sowcto that day.

In the cathedral, the switchboard operator called Tutu, who was in charge while the bishop of Johannesburg was away. She told him there were reports that children had been

Schoolchildren started a protest in 1976 against the use of the Afrikaans language in their schools. Here troop carriers roll into Soweto to confront demonstrators.

killed. Tutu called the army brigadier in charge of Soweto at the time and asked if children had been shot.

"Oh no, no, no," he replied, "the situation is under control."

"Have children been shot? And were they armed or anything like that?" Tutu asked again.

The brigadier said he was not going to answer questions from the public.

"Look, I'm not the public; I'm the vicar general of this diocese and I have every reason to know what is happening," Tutu retorted. The brigadier slammed down the phone.

Tutu got into a car with a fellow minister and drove near his house in Soweto, where they saw evidence of the riot. His response to the killing of children in Soweto was an anguished cry to the rest of the world: "For goodness' sake, somebody listen to us."

6

Speaking Out

Someone *was* listening after the Soweto shootings. People around the world condemned the violence used by the police against black children and youth. Whites in South Africa were shocked by the protest; it showed that blacks would no longer be timid in their opposition to apartheid. But the South African government cracked down even harder to try to contain the rebellion. Nelson Mandela had been sentenced to life imprisonment in 1963. Now his wife, Winnie Mandela, and Steve Biko, leader of the black consciousness movement, were arrested, along with many others.

As one of the few leaders left, Tutu was determined to speak out loud enough to be heard at home and to reach the world beyond South Africa. In 1976, Tutu was selected bishop of Lesotho, the small, independent country where he had once taught at the national university. He was only in Lesotho a year, however, before he was called back to the struggles in South Africa. He was offered a job as general secretary of the South African Council of Churches (SACC), a part of the World Council of Churches.

Young journalist Steve Biko founded the black consciousness movement in South Africa in the early 1970s. He inspired a generation of young blacks to pride and self-awareness. Anglican as a youth, he called on ministers like Tutu to help blacks' understanding of their value and worth.

When Tutu took charge in February 1978, the SACC was already unpopular. The Council represents 13 million Christians and all the main Protestant churches in South Africa, except the Baptists and the white branches of the Dutch Reformed church. It takes stands and works on major social issues for the member churches. Unfortunately for its relationship with the government, most of those social issues grow out of apartheid. Moreover, the SACC spends quite a bit of money to support its stands.

Besides educating a thousand high school students in rural areas, the Council gives scholarships for advanced schooling. It also helps more than six hundred families of political prisoners, banned persons, and migrant laborers. When the World Council of Churches gave money to the African National Congress, the money went through the SACC. Under Tutu's leadership, it became even more controversial.

When he accepted the job, Tutu was once again the "first black" in a job supervising both blacks and whites. Eighty percent of the Christians the SACC represents are black, but until 1970 most of its leaders were white. A Methodist layman, John Rees, had begun integrating the staff. He hired white secretaries for black administrators and black secretaries for white administrators, for example, equalized the salaries of black, Coloured, and white staff members, and desegregated the toilets. After five years, seven of the Council's thirteen full-time directors were black, and Rees resigned as general secretary in the hope that a black South African would succeed him.

When Tutu did, he lost no time letting everyone know where he stood. During his first year of leadership he gained a reputation as a fiery cleric who would "speak truth to power." Overcoming his short height with oratory, he put his message across with energy, humor, and joy. He did not hesitate to make connections between religion and politics, establishing a fund to pay legal costs for people accused of political offenses. Under his leadership he said the Council would work "for justice and peace and reconciliation," in that order.

One situation that begged for justice was the policy of forcing blacks to relocate in homelands assigned by the government. At times whole urban neighborhoods were destroyed and the inhabitants removed to dry, landlocked areas. It had happened to more than 3.5 million Africans.

Hearing reports of misery in the homelands, Tutu decided to see for himself. He visited a little girl who was living with her widowed mother and sister in the Ciskei. He asked the girl whether her mother received a pension or any other grant.

"No," she said.

"Then how do you live?" he asked.

"We borrow food," she replied.

"Have you ever returned food you borrowed?"

"No."

"What happens if you can't borrow food?"

"We drink water to fill our stomachs."

Tutu was haunted by the child's hunger and enraged by the government's policy. He accused the Nationalists of having a "final solution" for blacks, just as the Nazis had a final solution for the Jews—concentration camps and death.

"People are starving not because there isn't food but because of deliberate policy, and that in a country that boasts about its maize exports to Zambia!" If every white person in South Africa visited such a resettlement camp, he did not think they would support the policy.

To back up his strong words, Tutu directed SACC money to help two thousand Nyanga people defy a deportation order. As a result, they were able to return to their urban homes in the Eastern Cape in 1982. But he could not stop every relocation the government undertook. Government officials were angered by the "final solution" comment Tutu had made, but the controversy just made him more determined. "I will do all I can to destroy this diabolical system," he said as a guest speaker at a Methodist conference, "whatever the cost to me. I won't be stopped by anybody."

Preaching at funerals gave him an opportunity to speak to larger audiences. Since political gatherings are banned by the government, funerals are one of the few occasions when blacks can rally. One of his first was the funeral of Steve Biko, who had died in jail under suspicious circumstances. Later investigations showed Biko had been beaten.

Most Africans find urban living conditions (such as these in the Crossroads area of CapeTown) preferable to the homelands, where work is hard to find and the land is too barren to grow food.

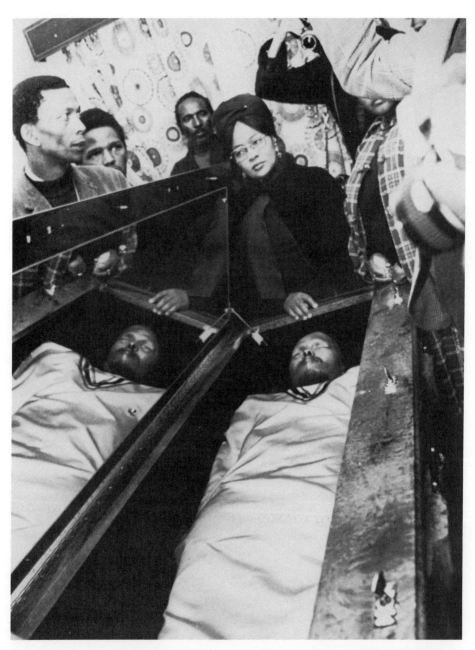

Ntsiki Biko, wife of Steve Biko, stands at the head of his coffin during the funeral. Biko was arrested in 1977 and died at the age of 31 of beatings he received from the police.

Six months later Tutu preached at a service for Robert Sobukwe, who had planned the 1960 demonstration against pass laws that ended in the Sharpeville massacre. When Sobukwe turned in his pass that day, he was arrested, imprisoned for nine years, and banned from speaking in public until the day he died. In his sermon, Tutu praised Sobukwe for his commitment to radical change without violence and bloodshed.

At times he continued to be just a simple pastor. While general secretary, he served as parish priest of St. Augustine's Church in part of Soweto. Although the church was plain, the service was anything but dull. The singing was fervent, the offering was a joyous parade to the altar, and during a part of the service called "passing of the peace," parishioners would surge through the sanctuary, smiling warmly, slapping hands, and embracing. Tutu gave the sermon at the center aisle, instead of from the elevated pulpit.

Weekdays he spent at the Council's offices in Johannesburg. Up early at 4:45 A.M. to run in Soweto, Tutu would drive to the cathedral for the Eucharist (communion) at 7:00 then to his SACC office at 8:00 for devotional readings and a quick look at the morning papers before staff prayers in the chapel at 8:30. The rest of the day was meetings, interviews, conferences, occasional luncheons, and tea breaks with his colleagues. On Wednesdays the staff prayed together for justice and reconciliation in the land. Some fasted on Thursdays for the same reason, and they celebrated communion once a month according to the rites of one of the member churches.

Such a multiracial, multidenominational irritation in the middle of Johannesburg did not go unnoticed. Prime Minister Vorster had warned the Council in 1968 against trying to do the kind of thing Martin Luther King, Jr., had done in America: ". . . the cloak you carry will not protect you if you try to do this in South Africa."

Indeed, in May 1980, one cloak-wearing colleague was arrested. Rev. John Thorne, a Coloured Congregational minister, had been general secretary for a short time before Tutu. He was detained without charge for addressing an "illegal" meeting in support of children boycotting classes.

When the council staff found out about his arrest, they immediately organized a demonstration, with Tutu in the lead. Thirty-five ministers carrying Bibles walked down a Johannesburg street toward John Vorster Square, where they were met by police in riot gear, carrying batons.

"Reverends, you are under arrest," cried the brigadier over a loudhailer, or bullhorn.

The reverends were taken to the police station, fingerprinted, photographed for the "rogues' gallery," and put in jail overnight. Lumped together in one cell, the ministers from different churches experienced something of church unity, a subject they had been talking about for years. When they appeared in court the next morning, they paid fines and were released. Thorne was released, too.

A year later another SACC director, Reverend Sol Jacobs, was arrested and detained. Then the government appointed a commission to investigate the SACC's finances. In five years the Council had received $10 million from churches, and the government wanted to know where it came from. They hoped to link Tutu and the SACC to a "web of subversive conspiracies facing South Africa." At least, they thought the investigation might intimidate Tutu or slow him down.

Keeping track of the budget was not Tutu's strength, but he was not easily intimidated either. When called to testify before the commission he didn't mince words: "Apartheid is as evil and as vicious as Nazism and communism," he told the Afrikaner officials. "The Government is not God, they are just ordinary human beings who very soon—like other tyrants before them—will bite the dust."

64

Bishop Tutu and Mrs. Leah Tutu leave court after spending a night in police custody. They were part of a demonstration against the arrest of Rev. John Thorne. Rev. Thorne was arrested for speaking at a meeting in support of children who were boycotting classes.

Strong words. When the commission issued a report, it criticized the amount of money the SACC spent for "political purposes" rather than for helping the needy and deserving. It denounced Tutu for some of the public statements he had made. But it did not ban the Council as it had banned the African National Congress and Pan-Africanist Congress.

So Tutu continued speaking out. Encouraged by the example of his white coworkers, he did not give up on whites. In 1980 he led a delegation from the Council to meet with the prime minister who had replaced Vorster, P. W. Botha. Tutu asked for a commitment from the government to end white rule. Botha asked Tutu to renounce any sympathy for underground movements like the ANC. Neither would agree to the other's requests.

Despite their disagreement, Tutu considered the meeting itself a miracle. It was the first time black leaders from outside the system had sat down with the prime minister. Moses went to Pharaoh several times, Tutu pointed out, even when he knew it was futile. "God does not give up on anybody. Not even P. W. Botha."

The more the government criticized Tutu, the more blacks supported him. Sobukwe, Biko, and ANC leader Chief Albert Luthuli, who had received the Nobel Prize for Peace in 1960, were dead. Mandela had been in jail for twenty years, and Tambo was in exile. Tutu felt he had become a leader by default.

By the end of his tenure at the SACC in 1984, his voice was well known. The man makes more speeches than he eats breakfasts, one editor wrote. Tutu agreed: "My wife and mother say, 'Why do you talk so much?' But I say if it's my destiny to speak out, I'd rather be happy in prison than unfree when I'm free."

7

"We Are Winning!"

Unable to keep the pesky priest quiet, the South African government seemed unsure what to do about him. The more Tutu spoke out, the more support he gained. The South African Council of Churches receives funds from many churches around the world. His position gave him the opportunity to speak to many of those churches.

Tutu used his trips abroad to challenge other countries' indirect support of apartheid. When he traveled to Europe in 1979 he told the Danes he found it rather disgraceful that Denmark was buying South African coal. He urged foreign countries to withdraw their business as a way of pressing an end to apartheid.

When his statement was reported in South Africa, some considered it treason. In retaliation, the government withheld his passport for a year when he returned. For the next few years, withdrawing his passport became the standard response. Sunday School children at St. James' Church in New York sent him "passports of love," which he pasted up on the walls of his office.

In 1981 he traveled abroad again, telling European and American audiences that their investments were helping "one of the most vicious systems since Nazism." He asked them to refuse to buy South African products such as gold and coal and to withdraw from doing business in the country. Economic pressure, he said, was the only way left to produce change without violence.

Gradually, he began to convince them. The Polaroid Company, for example, was selling the government equipment that it used to make the hated passes. Some of the company's American employees objected, and it stopped the sales.

People often asked him if economic pressure wouldn't hurt blacks more than whites, but Tutu replied, "It is no use being well-to-do when you are a slave."

Tutu is uniquely able to instill in white people an awareness of the hopes and aspirations of black people. Gavin Evans, for example, is the son of a white Anglican bishop in South Africa. As a high school exchange student in Texas, he described apartheid unfavorably when he was asked to speak. His Rotary Club sponsor heard about the talks and threatened to bring him home. Tutu wrote to Evans, whom he had met when he visited the Evans home, and encouraged him to keep speaking out. Buoyed by the letter, Evans refused to back down, and he was allowed to finish his year as an exchange student.

In addition to speaking engagements, two books of Tutu's sermons and essays were published by British and American publishers in 1982 and 1983. Many universities, including Harvard and Columbia, granted him honorary degrees. Since his passport had been impounded again, the president of Columbia came from New York to award the degree in person in 1982. When he was not allowed to go to Greece to accept the

Onassis Peace Prize, Tutu was cheerfully defiant. "There is nothing you can do which will stop us from becoming free!" he declared.

With her husband so much in the limelight, Leah Tutu had long been the anchor in the family, providing a normal family life amid an abnormal public life. Naomi recalls that her family was very much an African family when she was growing up, "but we grew up doing things that African children are not expected to do—such as speaking out and questioning authority."

Naomi and Mpho both went to college in the United States. Naomi married a fellow student at Berea College in

Bishop Tutu received the Martin Luther King, Jr. Peace Prize at Ebenezer Baptist Church in Atlanta, January 20, 1986. At left is Coretta Scott King and at right is Tutu's daughter Mpho. Christine King Farris, sister of Martin Luther King, Jr., drapes the medallion around Tutu.

Kentucky and earned a master's degree in international economic development. Trevor and Thandeka both work in Johannesburg.

With all four children gone from home, Leah became active in some of the same causes as Desmond. She was appointed a director of the South African Institute of Race Relations. She also worked for the SACC, trying to get the pay of household servants raised to $5 a day. Domestic workers, mainly black women, are not covered by the labor laws and receive no pensions or benefits.

In the fall of 1984, however, they both took a leave from work in South Africa. The couple went to New York, where Tutu taught for a semester at General Theological Seminary. His teaching was interrupted, however, in mid-October.

He slept badly the night of October 15. It reminded him of a night years ago when he was waiting for exam results. For the third time, he had been nominated for the Nobel Peace Prize, a prestigious award given every year by the Nobel Committee in Norway to a person known for peacemaking.

Early that morning, the chief Norwegian delegate to the United Nations came up the walk carrying a bouquet of bright yellow lilies, sky blue irises, and red zinnias, the colors of the Norwegian flag. Leah knew when she saw him that Desmond had won the prize for his efforts toward a peaceful end to apartheid.

Bells pealed at the seminary, and everyone gathered at the chapel, where Tutu read his favorite Psalm, the 139th. The Psalm says, in essence, "that I am nothing but the Lord's servant, that I go where He leads me and where He needs me."

The reaction in South Africa was joyous. Workers at the SACC office formed a gyrating human chain and danced through their offices. He and Leah flew back two days later to share the celebration.

The gold medal and $192,000 prize were awarded in a formal ceremony in Oslo, Norway, in November. Tutu received the award, he said, on behalf of all who had been working for a new society in South Africa. He used the money to start a scholarship fund for black African youths.

Most of all, however, the Nobel Prize was a morale booster. His first reaction on hearing of the award reflected that joy: "Hey, we are winning! Justice is going to win. . . . [It] means we mustn't give up." For a brief moment, at least, his side did seem to be winning.

The 1984 Nobel Peace Prize is awarded to Bishop Tutu in Oslo, Norway, by Egil Aarvik, chairman of the Nobel Peace Prize Committee. The award consists of a gold medal, a Nobel diploma, and $192,000.

A Vision for

South Africa

Once more, Desmond Tutu was preaching at the funeral of South Africans who had died fighting apartheid. This time the victims had been killed in an explosion of hand grenades, which they were apparently using to attack the homes of government employees. They thought the employees were cooperating with apartheid. Some mourners suggested that a police spy had given them faulty grenades to use.

The funeral was not just a service for friends and families but also a political gathering. A crowd of three thousand to four thousand people had come to the sports stadium in Duduza, a township thirty miles east of Johannesburg.

On this chilly winter day in July 1985, Tutu was a featured speaker. He had just become the first black Anglican bishop of Johannesburg. With his gray-tinged hair, gold-rimmed glasses, purple cassock, and silver cross, Bishop Tutu looked quite different from the mourners bundled up in an assortment of clothing. He was of a different generation, too, from the young men carrying the coffins. They wore yellow T-shirts with clenched fists or slogans like "Submit or fight."

During one of many funerals for blacks killed in riots in 1985, mourners carry a coffin to the cemetery. Their signs support the ANC and protest apartheid. UDF on their t-shirts stands for United Democratic Front, a coalition of antiapartheid groups.

Often on such occasions, the black, green, and gold banner of the ANC is unfurled. Songs are sung, like "God Bless Africa" or "Umkhonto we Sizwe" (Spear of the Nation). Many representatives from the community speak, and strong feelings are aroused. Then the procession moves through the streets of the township to the graveside.

As Bishop Tutu spoke, people became silent and craned their necks for a look at him. He urged the mourners not to use violent methods, and he described his hope for a future of peace with justice. Through their anger and frustration at the apartheid system, the mourners were still listening to a man of the church.

But as he stepped out of the cemetery after the burial, Tutu saw that the crowd had turned its fury on a man they thought was a police spy. They had overturned his car, set it on fire, and begun to beat him with clubs and whips, dousing him with gasoline and dragging him toward the flames.

Plunging into the crowd, Tutu cried that such mob actions undermine the liberation struggle. As he talked, the man was able to escape and stagger toward him. He was shoved into a car that sped away to safety. As some of the crowd chanted, "Guilty!" Tutu continued trying to reason with them.

This day Tutu was successful in preventing another violent death, but his argument for restraint is becoming harder to make. A twelve-year-old boy once challenged him. "Father, show me what you have achieved with all your talk of peaceful change, and I will show you what we gained with just a little violence."

There were many other funerals that year. Tutu had returned to South Africa from New York in January 1985, to a situation that was growing worse. The government had imposed a state of emergency for the first time since the Sharpeville shootings of 1960. Police were given great power to arrest and detain anyone they thought was causing trouble.

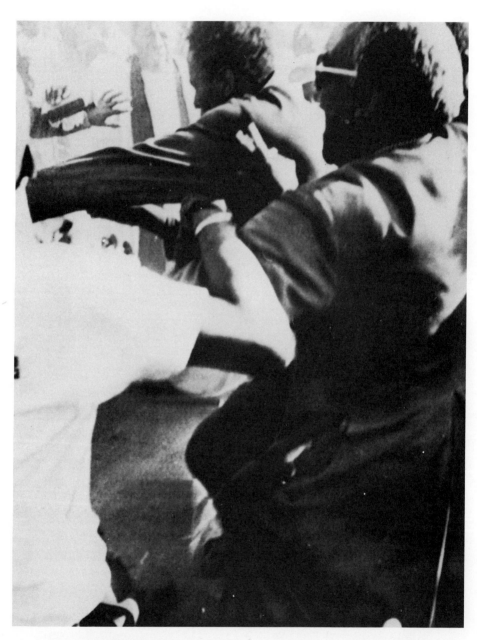

Bishop Tutu plunges into a crowd to rescue a man the crowd has attacked. The man was accused of being a spy for the police at the funeral. Tutu ordered the man carried to a nearby car and saved his life. Mob violence has claimed the lives of other blacks.

The church once again gave Tutu a broader pulpit from which to continue speaking out. Although the South African government was angered by the Nobel award, and many whites thought he was too political for a priest, the Anglican bishops had chosen him as the next bishop of Johannesburg. As bishop he would oversee the largest diocese in South Africa with 102 parishes and 300,000 church members, 80 percent of them black. Not long before, Africans had been only cleaners or tea makers in the diocesan offices.

Tutu was happy to be back in pastoral work: "I am fundamentally a pastor. . . . That's what God ordained me to do." He and Leah would remain in their Soweto home, rather than moving to the bishop's official residence in a whites-only suburb. Nor would he exercise the bishop's right to membership in the exclusively white Rand Club in the city. Rather, he would continue getting up early every morning to jog in Soweto and drive downtown for prayers in the cathedral and work at the diocesan offices.

In his consecration sermon, before a mixed-race congregation of 1,500 at St. Mary's, Bishop Tutu pledged to show his love for all his parishioners. To accomplish that goal, he took communion to Winnie Mandela, who was not allowed to leave her house. Winnie is the wife of Nelson Mandela, who was imprisoned for life in 1964. But Tutu also spoke at Afrikaner universities and to white congregations throughout Johannesburg, asking them, "Why can't we get together and make clear to authorities that we don't want our country destroyed by apartheid?" Many whites still saw him as an ogre because he was always talking about liberation.

Tutu responded that he was trying hard to be a bishop: "I manage with consummate skill to hide my horns, under my funny bishop's hat, and my tail tucked away under my trailing cape."

He was not one to cry "peace, peace" where there is no

peace, however. In the two years after he received the Nobel Prize, more than ten thousand people were arrested and at least two thousand blacks were killed, most by police.

"This government believes when people get obstreperous [rowdy], why just boink them one on the head and you will have sorted them out properly," Tutu complained.

He refused to condemn the ANC even when it began planting land mines and bombs. He will never tell someone to pick up a gun, he says, but he will "pray for the man who picks up the gun, pray that he will be less cruel than he might otherwise have been."

By conferring with a police officer at a funeral in Daveyton, Bishop Tutu eases a confrontation between mourners and the police. The South African Army had encircled the people at the funeral with armored cars, troops on horseback, and foot soldiers in order to prevent mob violence, but mourners saw them as a provocation.

Tutu says he is a peace lover but not a pacifist because he believes there are some situations where you have to fight. Nazism was one such situation; "apartheid could very well be another." Apartheid requires violence to enforce, he points out: a large police force, emergency decrees, and large-scale arrests. "When opponents of this system have challenged it nonviolently, they have gotten it in the neck for their pains." Many of the ANC members he knows were committed Christians who took up arms only when peaceful methods did not work.

Although what he says makes him unpopular, Tutu remains a moderate leader, a self-styled "teddy bear" between more radical black leaders and uncompromising Afrikaner leaders. He calls for an end to the state of emergency, withdrawal of troops from the townships, the release of political prisoners and the return of political exiles. Then all races in South Africa should sit down and talk.

His position in the middle is an uneasy one. The government warns him often that he is committing treason by calling for sanctions. Remembering his father's humiliation, he refuses to carry his pass. He, Leah, and his daughters have been searched; Leah and Naomi have been beaten; and Trevor was jailed for two weeks for talking back to a policeman. Nevertheless, his international stature and his high position in the church do seem to protect him from being detained or arrested or having his passport revoked.

In recent years, Tutu has been successful in influencing other countries' policies toward South Africa. The United States Congress and the Reagan administration imposed some sanctions on South Africa in 1986. Under pressure from apartheid opponents in the United States, many colleges, universities, and churches have sold the stock they owned in corporations that do business in South Africa.

Within South Africa, he continues to speak as a religious leader. At the age of fifty-five, he was elected to the highest position in the Anglican church in South Africa. He became the Archbishop of Cape Town in a ceremony at St. George's Cathedral in September 1986. In his lifetime an institution once run mainly by whites had chosen to put a black African at the controls.

Despite such changes within churches, however, whites in South Africa remain opposed to reforms. In the 1987 elections, the Nationalist party and P. W. Botha again won overwhelming support from white voters, prompting Tutu to comment, "We have entered the dark ages of the history of our country."

One of his first public actions as archbishop was to defy a new government prohibition. The prohibition bans opposition to the government's detention policy, under which thousands

Tutu became the Archbishop of Cape Town in September 1986. He takes communion after his enthronement at St. George's Cathedral. Tutu is the first black head of the Anglican church in South Africa.

of adults, youth, and children have been jailed without a trial. With other religious leaders conducting the service and with the United States ambassador in the congregation, Archbishop Tutu said he would not obey the order to keep quiet.

Opposing the government is a task Tutu would like to turn over to political leaders. If Nelson Mandela were released from prison, for example, Tutu says "it would be electric. For one thing, Bishop Tutu would get on with his work of being bishop, man." He has predicted that Mandela or a similar black leader will be prime minister by the end of the 1980s.

With those leaders in jail or in exile, however, his mission in the coming years is to see that black liberation from apartheid comes peacefully. In months of funerals and violent confrontations in the 1980s, Tutu's message remained the same: justice, peace, and reconciliation, **in that order.**

If Nelson Mandela were released from prison, "it would be electric," Tutu says. He clasps the hand of Nelson's daughter, Zindzi Mandela, after she has read a statement by her father in which he refused to accept President P.W. Botha's offer. Botha offered to release Mandela if he would promise not to use violence to end apartheid.

Sometimes he gets discouraged and wants to pack up and leave the country. "You get to feel sorry for yourself and say, 'Is it worth it to try to prevent major tragedies? Is there any point anymore?'" His own vision of the future is like the multiracial services at St. Mary's Cathedral. South Africa would have a democratic government, a majority government, and a black president. It would be a more compassionate, caring society.

During a trip to the United States in 1987, Tutu gave the commencement address at Oberlin College, the first college in the United States to admit black students. His message was not new, but he said it once again: peace in South Africa will come through the efforts of "black and white together, black and white together." He only hopes he is heard before time runs out for a peaceful solution.

Tutu prays that blacks and whites together will bring a peaceful solution to the violent separation between the races in South Africa.

Chronology

Year	Event
1931	Born in Klerksdorp, a gold mining-town west of Johannesburg
1938	Family moves to Ventersdorp; starts school at St. Ansgars
1943	Family moves to Johannesburg
1944	Starts high school at Madibane (Western Native) High School
1945	Ill with tuberculosis; visited by Father Huddleston
1948	Nationalists elected to government; pass apartheid laws
1950	Graduated from Madibane; enrolls at Bantu Normal College
1952	ANC organizes Defiance Campaign against apartheid laws
1954	Receives B.A. from University of Johannesburg; starts teaching at Madibane High School

1955	Marries Leah Nomalizo Shenxane; teaches at Munsieville High School; Sophiatown is removed by South African government
1957	Resigns from teaching as Bantu Education Act goes into effect; begins training for priesthood, Anglican Church
1960	Sharpeville massacre
1961	Ordained as a priest
1962	Goes to King's College in London, England; Nelson Mandela arrested for plotting sabotage
1964	Nelson Mandela sentenced to life imprisonment
1966	After receiving B.A. and Master's in Theology, returns to South Africa
1967	Lecturer at Federal Theological Seminary
1970	Lecturer at National University of Lesotho
1972	Returns to England to work for the World Council of Churches
1975	Named first black dean of Johannesburg
1976	Soweto riots
1978	Becomes Secretary General of the South African Council of Churches; Steve Biko dies of beating in prison
1980	Meets with Prime Minister Botha
1984	Awarded Nobel Peace Prize
1985	Enthroned as Bishop of Johannesburg
1986	Installed as Archbishop of Cape Town

Glossary

African National Congress (ANC)—An organization formed in 1912 to oppose white domination in South Africa

Afrikaans—The language spoken by descendants of the Dutch in South Africa; an older form of Dutch with many words adopted from African languages

Afrikaner—A descendant of the Dutch, German, or French Huguenot settlers

Anglican—A member of the Anglican Communion, the Church of England and its related churches in other countries such as South Africa

apartheid—A system of laws that separates the races and puts whites in a superior position

archbishop—The highest-ranking bishop; in South Africa, the bishop who presides over all of the Anglican churches in the country

Bantu—A word commonly used by white South Africans to describe a black African

bishop—A high-ranking priest who supervises other priests and a church district

black consciousness—A feeling of pride and self-respect in being black

black theology—A system of beliefs that says Christianity promises freedom to blacks

Coloured—In South Africa, a person of mixed race

deacon—The rank just below priest in the Anglican church

dean—The Anglican priest who presides at a cathedral and supervises a number of parishes in a diocese

diocese—The district supervised by a bishop

Dutch Reformed Church—The main Protestant church to which Afrikaners belong

Eucharist—A service of communion

homeland—An area set aside for blacks to live in outside of urban areas

Kaffir—A derogatory word for a black African

location—An area outside of a town or city where blacks are allowed to live

Nationalists—A political party dominated by Afrikaners that has been in control of the government since 1948

Native—A European word for native black African

Pan-Africanist Congress—An organization started by Robert Sobukwe to protest the pass laws

parish—A district of a church under the charge of a priest or minister

priory—The place where members of a religious order, such as the Community of the Resurrection, live

Rand—*See* Witwatersrand

seminary—A school or college where persons are trained to become priests, ministers, or rabbis

separate development—A term used by the government to replace *apartheid*

Sotho—Language spoken by the Tswana and other tribes

South African Council of Churches—An organization of most of the Protestant churches in South Africa that exists to take a common stand on major social issues

township—*See* location

Tswana—An African tribe known for settling disputes through peaceful negotiation

umfundisi—A preacher

vicar general—A deputy to a bishop

Witwatersrand—A ridge of mountains; *witwaters* means "white water" and describes the light color of the water that runs off the sides of the hills following the summer rains

World Council of Churches—An organization representing most of the Protestant churches in the world

Xhosa—The second largest African tribe in South Africa; they fought a long series of wars with the white settlers

Further Reading

Huddleston, Trevor. *Naught for Your Comfort*. Garden City, New York: Doubleday & Co., Inc., 1956.

Laure, Jason. *South Africa: Coming of Age under Apartheid*. New York: Farrar, Straus, Giroux, 1980.

Lawson, Don. *South Africa*. New York: Franklin Watts, 1986.

Lelyveld, Joseph. *Move Your Shadow: South Africa Black and White*. New York: Times Books, 1985.

Magubane, Peter. *Black Child*. New York: Knopf, 1982.

Mandela, Winnie. *A Part of My Soul Went with Him*. New York: W. W. Norton, Inc., 1985.

Mathabane, Mark. *Kaffir Boy: The True Story of a Black Youth's Coming of Age in Apartheid South Africa*. New York: Macmillan, 1986.

Meyer, Carolyn. *Voices of South Africa: Growing up in a Troubled Land*. Orlando, Fla.: Gulliver Books, Harcourt Brace Jovanovich, 1986.

Naidoo, Beverley. *Journey to Jo'burg: A South African Story*. New York: J.B. Lippincott, 1985.

Paton, Alan. *Ah, but Your Land Is Beautiful*. New York: Scribner, 1981.

Tutu, Desmond. *Crying in the Wilderness: The Struggle for Justice in South Africa*. Introduced and edited by John Webster. Grand Rapids, Mich.: Wm. B. Eerdmans Publishing Co., 1982.

Tutu, Desmond. *Hope and Suffering, a collection of sermons and addresses*. Grand Rapids, Mich.: Wm. B. Eerdmans Publishing Co., 1983.

Index

96